This Little Tiger book belongs to:

____

____

____

For Reg and Muriel ~ E B

Here's hoping we all find our own pot of gold ~ C P

LITTLE TIGER PRESS
An imprint of Magi Publications
1 The Coda Centre, 189 Munster Road, London SW6 6AW
www.littletigerpress.com

First published in Great Britain 2008
This edition published 2009

A CIP catalogue record for this book is available from the British Library.

 • ISBN 978-1-84506-639-0

Printed in China

10 9 8 7 6 5 4 3 2 1

Little Pip and the Rainbow Wish

Elizabeth Baguley

Caroline Pedler

LITTLE TIGER PRESS
London

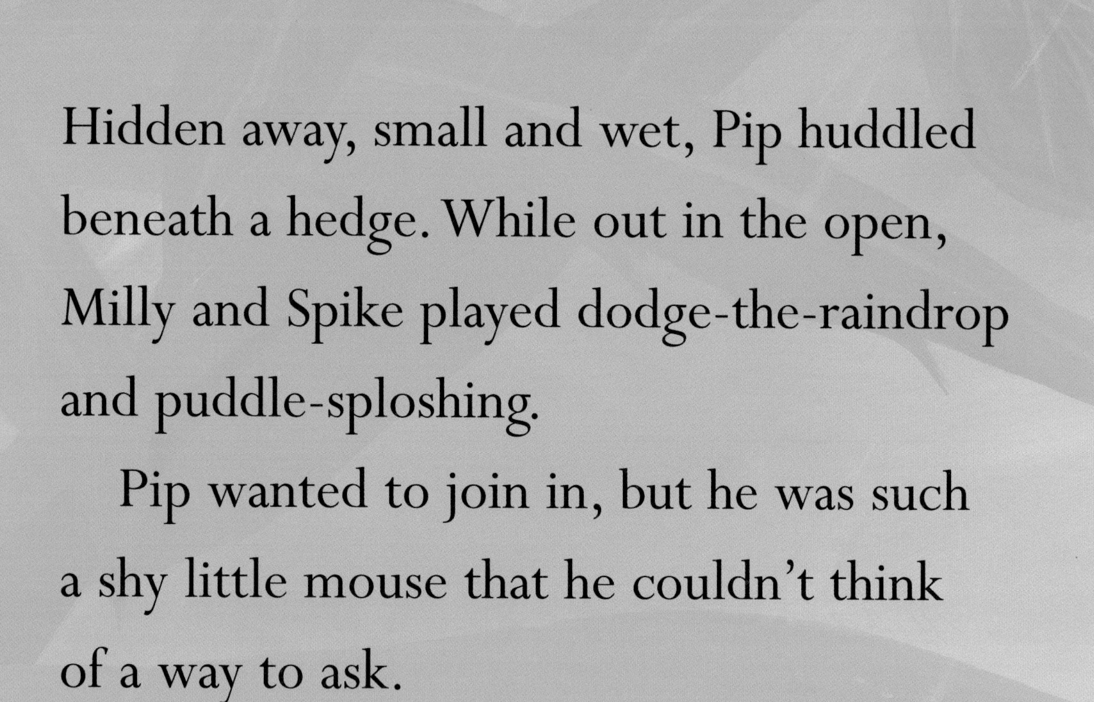

Hidden away, small and wet, Pip huddled beneath a hedge. While out in the open, Milly and Spike played dodge-the-raindrop and puddle-sploshing.

Pip wanted to join in, but he was such a shy little mouse that he couldn't think of a way to ask.

Pip watched as Spike
gave Milly a dandelion clock.
Together they wiggled and
whooped around it. Perhaps,
Pip thought, if I had
something to give them,
they would play with *me*.
He looked around him but
could see only scratchy
stones and patchy sky.

Just at that moment . . .

. . . a shining rainbow lit up the clouds. What a present *that* would be for Milly and Spike! They could slide down it, balance on it, make a tent under its colours. And he would be their friend.

But the rainbow was so far away . . .

. . . too high to reach on
the tips of his paws . . .

too far away to catch
with a bendy stick . . .

and his bounce was
just not bouncy enough.

No matter what he tried,
the rainbow was very, very up
and Pip was very, very down.

“What are you doing?” asked Milly,
who had stopped playing to watch.

Pip's tail blushed to its very tip.
"I wanted to catch the . . . er . . . er . . ."
"The rainbow?" said Spike. "That's brilliant! We'll help!"

Spike clambered onto Milly's shoulders.

"Come on, Pip," he called. "We need you, too." And he swung Pip right to the top of the mouse-tower.

The tower was sky-high. But then Pip began to wobble . . . the tower began to sway . . .

And

they

all

fell

into

a

jumbly

mouse

heap!

"We could just *wish* for the rainbow," Pip said, quietly.

"Good idea!" said Spike, and together they squeezed their wish into the sky.

But the rainbow stayed just where it was.

Then Milly picked up the dandelion clock. “Someone could fly to the rainbow!” she said. “Who’s lightest?”

“Me, me!” cried Pip, suddenly not shy at all.

Milly and Spike pulled Pip along, until the wind scooped him up so high that he could almost touch the rainbow.

He reached out his paws. But the seeds began to fall from the dandelion clock, one . . .

by one . . .

by one.

And

Pip

sank

s l o w l y

back

to

earth.

"I didn't catch the rainbow," said Pip, sadly.

"You were very brave," said Milly, hugging him.

"We'll just have to think of another way," said Spike.

But at that very moment, the rain dripped to a stop and the rainbow melted away and was gone.

"Don't go!" begged Pip. "Please don't go!"

"Don't worry," said Spike. "There'll be another rainbow."

"But I needed it," sniffed Pip. "To give to you and Milly, so that you would be my friends."

"But we *are* your friends!" said Milly.

"Who needs presents anyway?" said Spike.

Then off they raced, all together, hopping and sploshing from puddle to puddle, until the night sky burst into a brilliant sparkling of stars.

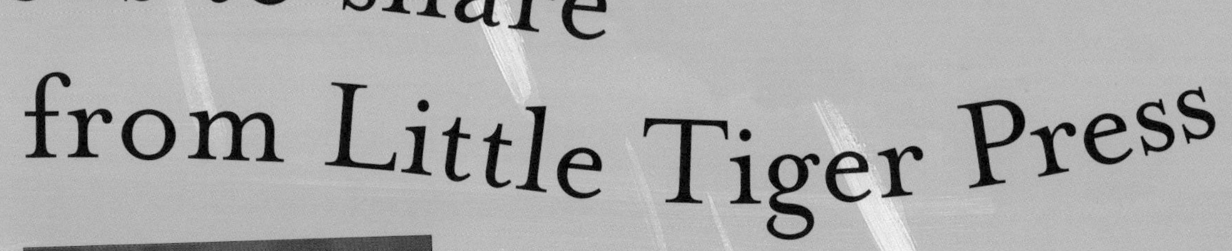
More books to share
from Little Tiger Press

Gillian Lobel
Little Honey Bear and the Smiley Moon
Tim Warnes

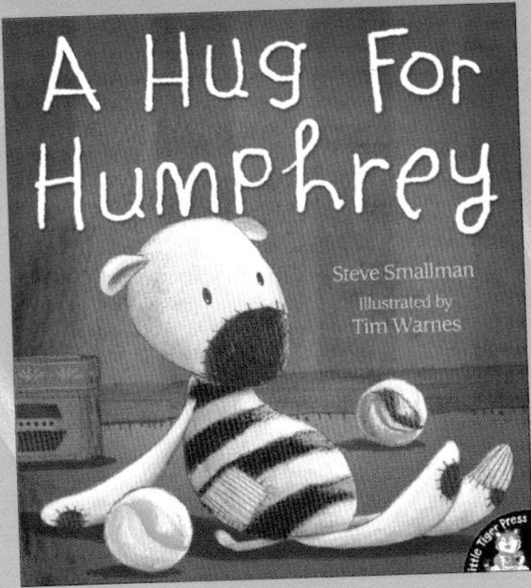
A Hug For Humphrey
Steve Smallman
Illustrated by Tim Warnes

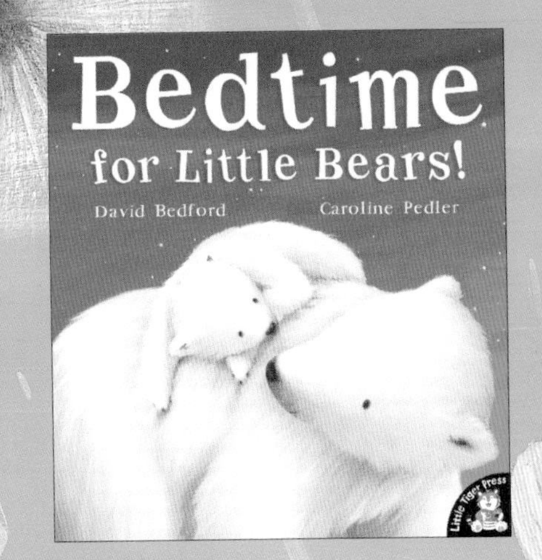
Bedtime for Little Bears!
David Bedford
Caroline Pedler

AUGUSTUS AND HIS SMILE
CATHERINE RAYNER

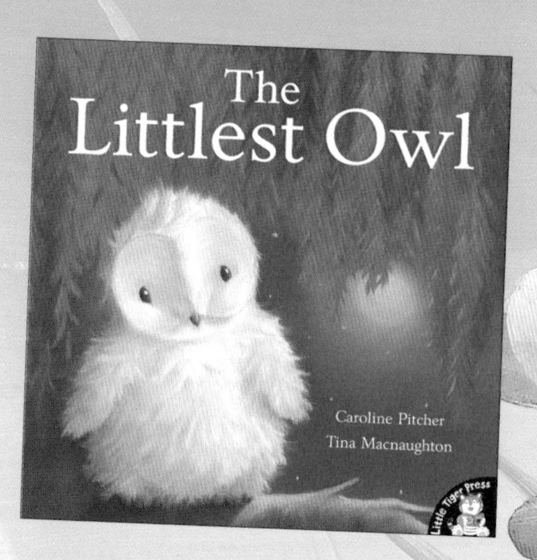
The Littlest Owl
Caroline Pitcher
Tina Macnaughton

The Most Precious Thing
Gill Lewis
Louise Ho

For information regarding any of the above titles
or for our catalogue, please contact us:
Little Tiger Press, 1 The Coda Centre,
189 Munster Road, London SW6 6AW
Tel: 020 7385 6333 Fax: 020 7385 7333
E-mail: info@littletiger.co.uk
www.littletigerpress.com